I0663263

The Young Tsar

*Absolute Power, Moral Awakening,
and the Burden of Leadership*

A Modern Translation

Adapted for the Contemporary Reader

Leo Tolstoy

Translated by Tim Zengerink

© Copyright 2025
All rights reserved.

It is not legal to reproduce, duplicate, or transmit any part of this document in either electronic means or in printed format. Recording of this publication is strictly prohibited and any storage of this document is not allowed unless with written permission from the publisher except for the use of brief quotations in a book review.

This book contains works of fiction. Any resemblance to persons living or dead, or places, events, or locations is purely coincidental.

Table of Contents

Preface - Message to the Reader

What If You Could Help Rebuild the Greatest Library in Human History?

Thousands of years ago, the Library of Alexandria stood as the crown jewel of human achievement — a sanctuary where the collected wisdom of every known civilization was gathered, preserved, and shared freely.

And then, it was lost.

Through fire, conquest, and the slow erosion of time, humanity lost not just books — but ideas, dreams, discoveries, and stories that could have changed the world forever.

Today, the Library of Alexandria lives again — and you are invited to be a part of its restoration.

Our mission is simple yet profound:

To rebuild the greatest library the world has ever known, and to translate all timeless works into every language and dialect, so that no seeker of knowledge is ever left behind again.

By joining our movement to rebuild the modern Library of Alexandria, you become part of an unprecedented mission:

- **Unlimited Access to the Greatest Audiobooks & eBooks Ever Written:**

  Instantly explore thousands of legendary works—Plato, Shakespeare, Jane Austen, Leo Tolstoy, and countless more. All instantly available to read or listen, placing a complete literary universe at your fingertips.

- **Beautiful Paperback & Deluxe Editions at Printing Cost**

  Own any title as an elegant paperback, deluxe hardcover, or stunning collectible boxset—offered to you at true printing cost, delivered straight to your door. Build your personal Library of Alexandria, crafted for beauty, built for durability, and worthy of proud display.

- **Fresh Translations for Modern Readers—in Every Language & Dialect**

  Enjoy timeless masterpieces reimagined in clear, contemporary language—no more outdated phrases or obscure references. Alongside the original versions, we're tirelessly translating these classics into every language and dialect imaginable, ensuring accessibility and understanding across cultures and generations.

- **Join a Global Renaissance of Literature & Knowledge**

  You directly support expanding our library, publishing deluxe editions at true cost, translating works into all global languages, and bringing humanity's greatest stories to people everywhere. By joining today, you're not just preserving a legacy of masterpieces; you set in motion a powerful wave of literary accessibility.

Become a Torchbearer of Knowledge.

Join us for free now at **LibraryofAlexandria.com**

Together, we will ensure that the light of human wisdom never fades again.

With gratitude and a shared love of knowledge,

The Modern Library of Alexandria Team

Visit:

www.libraryofalexandria.com

Or scan the code below:

Introduction

Power, Conscience, and
the Awakening of a Sovereign Soul

Leo Tolstoy's The Young Tsar is a short but potent story that examines one of the most timeless and volatile questions in human society: What happens when absolute power is placed in the hands of someone morally sincere but ethically unprepared? Written in 1894, shortly after the coronation of Nicholas II, The Young Tsar was deemed so politically sensitive that it remained unpublished in Russia until years after Tolstoy's death. In it, Tolstoy explores the internal transformation of a newly crowned monarch who, upon encountering the brutal realities of the state he governs, undergoes a profound moral awakening.

The story captures the essence of Tolstoy's late-life moral and political philosophy. By the time he wrote The Young Tsar, Tolstoy had renounced organized religion, aristocratic privilege, and traditional notions of state power. He had come to embrace a radically nonviolent, ethical Christianity that viewed institutional authority—especially the state, the military, and the church—as morally compromised and spiritually corrupting. This story, though fictional, is imbued with Tolstoy's own anxieties about leadership, justice, and human suffering. It offers not only a poignant critique of imperial authority, but also a hopeful vision of moral awakening and personal responsibility.

The central character, the young tsar himself, begins the story as a confident, idealistic ruler, eager to do good. However, through a series of revelations—often prompted by divine insight or conscience—he begins to see the gulf between his intentions and the effects of the political machinery he controls. He learns about capital punishment, military conscription, judicial cruelty, and the everyday violence that props up the empire. These realizations shake him to his core. What follows is not a public revolution but a spiritual one: a quiet internal rebellion against inherited power, custom, and cruelty.

Tolstoy does not portray the young tsar as evil or tyrannical. Rather, he is naive—a product of privilege and flattery, unaware of how detached he is from the lives of those he rules. In that sense, the story is not just about monarchy—it is about any form of leadership, and about the awakening that must occur when power meets moral truth.

The Silent Cry of the People:
State Violence and the Illusion of Authority

One of the most striking features of The Young Tsar is its presentation of violence—not as spectacle, but as silence. The suffering of the people under the tsar's rule is not seen directly; it is uncovered gradually, through moments of reflection, report, and conscience. In this way, Tolstoy exposes the structural violence of an imperial regime: it is not made of atrocities alone, but of bureaucracy, neglect, and ignorance. The tsar, in his palace, surrounded by advisors and officials, is unaware of the brutal consequences of the policies he passively endorses. It is only through introspection, prayer, and moral imagination that he begins to grasp the truth.

Tolstoy structures the story around a series of moral discoveries. The young tsar is confronted with the realities of corporal punishment, forced military service, imprisonment, and the execution of innocent men. Each revelation pushes him further into self-doubt. At first, he believes he can fix things from above—by issuing reforms, choosing better officials, or changing policy. But Tolstoy leads him (and the reader) to a deeper realization: that no structure of absolute power, no matter how well-intentioned, can produce true justice. Justice, in Tolstoy's view, comes only from personal moral action—from love, truth, and voluntary sacrifice.

This insight is not only spiritual, but deeply political. Tolstoy's critique of the tsar is not a call for a better monarch—it is a rejection of monarchy itself. He saw in all coercive institutions the seeds of moral corruption. Through the figure of the tsar, he dramatizes the cost of unexamined power. The young ruler's growing torment is the necessary pain of conscience awakening to the truth. His crisis is universal: it is the challenge of every leader, every citizen, and every soul who must ask, "What am I responsible for? What does my power cost others?"

Tolstoy does not offer an easy resolution. The story ends not with political change, but with a turning inward. The tsar begins to question not just his administration, but the entire basis of his authority. He contemplates the teachings of Christ, particularly the call to love one's neighbor and to renounce violence. In this, he mirrors Tolstoy's own journey—away from wealth, power, and prestige, and toward a life of ethical humility.

This modern translation aims to capture the clarity, conviction, and quiet urgency of Tolstoy's original prose while making its language accessible to contemporary readers. Every effort has been made to retain the emotional and spiritual arc of the young tsar's journey while highlighting the enduring relevance of Tolstoy's moral vision.

In conclusion, The Young Tsar is not merely a political critique or a historical allegory. It is a parable of conscience—one that speaks to any age, any leader, and any reader who has ever wondered what it truly means to be good in a world built on injustice. Tolstoy's story reminds us that true leadership is not about control, but about compassion. It is not about issuing orders, but about bearing witness to suffering—and doing everything in one's power to stop it. In an era when power often shields itself from accountability, The Young Tsar remains a quiet but radical call to moral awakening.

The Young Tsar

The young Tsar had recently become ruler. For five weeks, he had been working non-stop, doing everything a leader was expected to do. He read reports, signed papers, met with ambassadors and important officials, and inspected his soldiers. He was completely worn out. Like a traveler desperate for water and rest after a long trip, he wished for just one day without meetings, speeches, or ceremonies. He just wanted a few hours to relax and be himself with his young, smart, and beautiful wife, whom he had married only a month ago.

It was Christmas Eve, and the Tsar had planned to finally rest that evening. The night before, he had stayed up late going through important documents from his ministers. That morning, he attended a church service and then a military ceremony. In the afternoon, he met with government officials, and later, he had to listen to reports from three different ministers.

With the Minister of Finance, he agreed to raise taxes on imported goods, which would bring millions more into the country's budget. He also approved the Crown's sale of brandy in certain regions and allowed alcohol sales in market villages, increasing the government's revenue from alcohol sales. He approved a new gold loan for financial purposes.

The Minister of Justice presented a complicated inheritance case involving Baron Snyders, and the Tsar confirmed the final decision. He also signed new rules about Article 1830 of the penal code, which punished vagrants.

When he met with the Minister of the Interior, he approved the collection of overdue taxes, signed an order about how to handle religious dissenters, and agreed to extend martial law in certain regions. With the Minister of War, he discussed the appointment of a new Corps Commander, the recruitment of new soldiers, and how to discipline those who disobeyed military rules.

These tasks kept him busy until dinner, and even then, he wasn't free. Important officials had been invited, and he had to talk to them—not in the way he wanted, but in the way they expected. Finally, the long and exhausting dinner ended, and the guests left.

The young Tsar let out a deep sigh of relief, stretched his arms, and headed to his private room to take off his heavy uniform with all its medals. He changed into a comfortable jacket he used to wear before becoming ruler. His wife also left to change out of her fancy dress, telling him she would be back soon.

As he walked past the row of footmen standing at attention and entered his room, he felt a deep sense of freedom. Taking off the heavy uniform and putting on his jacket made him feel lighter, filling his heart with warmth and happiness. He stretched out on the sofa, resting his head on his hand while staring at the dim glow of the lamp. A drowsy feeling, one he hadn't experienced since childhood, slowly washed over him.

"My wife will be here soon and will find me asleep. No, I must stay awake," he told himself. But as he adjusted his position, enjoying the peaceful moment, sleep took over without him even realizing it. He drifted off completely, unaware of when or how it happened.

He didn't know how long he had been asleep when he suddenly felt a soft touch on his shoulder.

"She's here," he thought. "I can't believe I dozed off."

But when he opened his eyes, it wasn't his wife standing before him. Instead, a man was there. The Tsar had never seen him before, yet somehow, he felt as if he had known him for a long time. There was no fear or confusion—only a strange sense of trust, as if this meeting was meant to happen.

"Come," said the stranger.

"Yes, let's go," said the young Tsar, though he had no idea where they were going. Still, he knew he had no choice but to follow the stranger. "But how will we get there?" he asked.

"Like this."

The stranger placed his hand on the Tsar's head, and suddenly, everything went dark. He couldn't tell how long he had been unconscious, but when he came to, he found himself in an unfamiliar place.

The first thing he noticed was the overwhelming stench, thick and suffocating, like rotting sewage. He stood in a wide hallway dimly lit by the red glow of two weak lamps. On one side, there was a thick wall with barred windows. On the other, heavy doors with large locks. A soldier stood nearby, leaning against the wall, asleep.

The young Tsar could hear the faint, muffled sounds of people—not just one or two, but many— coming from behind the doors. The stranger beside him placed a gentle but firm hand on his shoulder and guided him toward the first door, as if the guard wasn't even there. The young Tsar felt powerless to resist and stepped closer.

To his surprise, the soldier looked right at him but didn't react. He didn't straighten up or salute. Instead, he let out a loud yawn and scratched the back of his neck as if he couldn't see the Tsar at all.

The door had a small peephole. The stranger's hand nudged him forward, urging him to look inside. The terrible smell made him hesitate, but the push was firm. He leaned in and peered through the hole.

The sight before him was so shocking that he forgot the stench.

Inside a cramped, filthy room, about ten yards long and six yards wide, men paced back and forth without stopping. Some wore long gray coats, some had felt boots, and others were barefoot. There were more than twenty men in the room, but at first, the Tsar only focused on those walking. They moved quickly, silently, their steps sharp and repetitive, turning as soon as they reached the walls, never looking at each other, lost in their own thoughts.

The young Tsar had seen something similar before—once, at a zoo, he had watched a tiger pacing in its cage, moving back and forth with the same restless energy, its tail flicking, its eyes empty, trapped in endless motion.

He examined the prisoners more closely. One young man, likely a peasant, had curly hair and could have been handsome, but his face was pale and his eyes burned with something dark and inhuman. Another man, a bearded Jew, stood silently with a gloomy expression. An older prisoner, thin and bald, had a rough beard, as if he had once been clean-shaven but had since let it grow out in uneven patches. Another was tall and broad-shouldered, with thick muscles, a sloped forehead, and a flat nose. There was also a sickly, thin boy, barely more than a child, who looked too weak to even be standing. The last was a small, wiry man who twitched and muttered to himself, moving as if he was skipping rather than walking.

The Tsar watched them with intense curiosity, studying their faces, their movements, the way they avoided eye contact. Then he noticed the others in the room—some standing off to the side, some lying on a raised wooden platform that served as a bed. Near the door, he saw a bucket—the source of the horrible stench.

On the platform, about ten men lay curled up under thin blankets. One of them, a red-haired man with a thick beard, was sitting up, inspecting his shirt under the dim light, searching for lice. Another prisoner, an old man with snow-white hair, stood near the wall, crossing himself over and over, deeply focused on his prayers, as if the filth and suffering around him didn't exist.

"This must be a prison," thought the young Tsar. "It's terrible. They deserve pity. But this is their own doing. They wouldn't be here if they hadn't broken the law."

But as soon as the thought crossed his mind, the stranger beside him responded, as if he had heard it.

"They are all locked up here because of your orders. They were all sentenced in your name. But most of them are not worse than you or the people who judged them. In fact, many of them are better. Look at this one." The stranger pointed to the young man with curly hair. "He's a murderer, but no more guilty than those who kill in war or in duels and get rewarded for it. He had no education, no one to guide him, and he grew up surrounded by thieves and drunks. That doesn't excuse him, but it explains why he ended up like this. He killed a merchant to rob him.

"The other man, the Jew, is a thief, part of a gang. The strong one over there stole a horse, which is a crime, but not the worst compared to others. Watch."

Suddenly, the young Tsar found himself in an open field near a border. To the right, there were potato fields with plants dug up and left in frozen heaps. Beyond them were fields of winter crops and, in the distance, a small village with tiled roofs. On the left, there were more fields and patches of stubble. The land was empty except for a single black figure standing at the border with a rifle slung over his back, a dog by his side.

Near where the Tsar stood, sitting just at his feet, was a young Russian soldier with a green band on his cap and a rifle on his shoulder. He was rolling a piece of paper to make a cigarette. The soldier didn't seem to notice the Tsar or his guide and didn't react when the Tsar, standing right above him, asked, "Where are we?"

"On the Prussian border," the guide answered.

Suddenly, a gunshot rang out in the distance. The soldier jumped to his feet. He saw two men running, crouched low to the ground. Quickly shoving his tobacco back into his pocket, he took off after one of them.

"Stop, or I'll shoot!" the soldier shouted.

The man kept running but turned his head to yell something back—probably an insult.

"Curse you!" the soldier growled, planting his foot forward. He aimed his rifle, adjusted his sight, and fired. The Tsar heard no sound, but he assumed the soldier was using smokeless powder. He watched as the fleeing man staggered forward, taking a few more steps before collapsing. He tried to crawl, but soon he lay still.

The second man, who had been running ahead, turned back, crouched beside the fallen man for a moment, then took off again.

"What just happened?" the Tsar asked.

"That was a border guard doing his job," the guide replied. "The man was shot to protect the government's money."

"Is he really dead?"

The guide placed his hand on the Tsar's head again, and once more, the Tsar lost consciousness.

When he woke up, he was inside a small customs office. A man's dead body lay on the floor. He had a thin, graying beard, a sharp nose, and closed eyes. His arms were stretched out, and his bare feet stuck up stiffly. His side had a gunshot wound, and his ragged jacket and blue shirt were covered in dark, dried blood, with a few fresh red stains.

A woman stood against the wall, wrapped in layers of shawls, her face barely visible. She stared at the dead man's face, his upturned feet, his lifeless eyes. Every few moments, she sobbed, wiped her tears, then fell silent again. A young girl, about thirteen, stood beside her, her mouth and eyes wide open. A boy, no older than eight, clung to his mother's skirt, staring intensely at his father's lifeless body without blinking.

A door opened, and several men entered—an official, an officer, a doctor, and a clerk carrying documents. Behind them came the soldier who had fired the shot. At first, he walked with confidence, but as soon as he saw the dead man, he went pale and froze in place. He lowered his head and stood there, trembling.

The official asked him, "Is this the man who was crossing the border when you shot him?"

The soldier's lips quivered. His face twitched as he struggled to speak. "S-s-s…" he stammered, unable to finish. Then, barely above a whisper, he forced out the words: "Yes, sir."

The officials exchanged glances and wrote something down.

"You see what comes from this system?" the guide said.

The scene changed again. Now, the Tsar was inside a richly decorated room where two men sat drinking wine. One was old and gray, the other a young Jewish man. The younger one held a thick roll of banknotes, bargaining with the older man. He was buying smuggled goods.

"You got them cheap," the younger man said with a smirk.

"Yes," the old man replied. "But the risk…"

"This is awful," the young Tsar said. "But it can't be avoided. These things are necessary."

The stranger said nothing, only replied, "Let's keep going," and placed his hand on the Tsar's head again.

When the Tsar opened his eyes, he was in a small room dimly lit by a lamp. A woman sat at a table sewing. A boy, about eight years old, was drawing, curled up in an armchair with his legs tucked under him. A young man was reading aloud. Just then, a man and a young woman entered the room, laughing loudly.

"You signed the order allowing the sale of alcohol," the guide said.

"So, what happened?" the woman asked.

"He won't make it," the young man replied.

"What's wrong with him?"

"They kept him drunk the whole time."

"That can't be true!" the woman gasped.

"It is. And he's only nine—Vania Moroshkine."

"Did you try to save him?" she asked.

"I did everything I could. Gave him medicine to make him sick, put a mustard plaster on him… but he has all the signs of alcohol poisoning."

"That family has always been full of drunks," the young woman said. "Annisia is the only one who's a little better, but even she's usually drunk."

"And what about your temperance group?" the student asked his sister.

"What can we do when they're given every chance to drink? Father tried to shut down the tavern, but the law protects it. And when I told Vasily Ermiline that selling alcohol was ruining people, he just laughed and said, 'I have a license with the Imperial eagle on it. If it was wrong, the Tsar wouldn't have allowed it.' Isn't that awful? The whole village has been drunk for three days. And on holidays, it's even worse!

"We already know that alcohol doesn't do any good—it only causes harm. It's been proven to be nothing but poison. Most crimes happen because of it. In other countries, like Sweden and Finland, when drinking was banned, life got better. People became healthier and acted more responsibly. But in our country, the people who could make a difference—the government, the Tsar, and his officials—do the opposite. They encourage drinking because it brings in money. Even they drink! They make toasts at every event—'To the regiment!' The priests drink, even the bishops…"

Once again, the guide touched the Tsar's head, and everything changed.

The Tsar found himself inside a peasant's home. A man, about forty years old, his face red and his eyes bloodshot, was wildly beating an elderly man who struggled to defend himself.

"Stop! You're hitting your own father!" someone cried.

"I don't care! I'll kill him! Let them send me to Siberia, I don't care!" the man shouted.

Women screamed as drunk officials stormed in, dragging the two men apart. The older man's arm was broken, and the younger one had chunks of his beard ripped out. Nearby, a drunken girl was throwing herself at an old, equally drunk peasant.

"They're like animals!" the young Tsar whispered in horror.

The guide touched his head again.

This time, the Tsar was in a courtroom. A fat, bald judge with a heavy gold chain around his neck stood up and read a sentence in a loud voice. Behind a wooden railing, a group of peasants stood, their faces full of worry. A woman in ragged clothes sat slumped over, unmoving. A guard kicked her.

"Get up! Pay attention!" he barked.

Slowly, the woman stood.

"By order of His Imperial Majesty..." the judge began reading. She had been caught taking half a bundle of oats from a landowner's field. The sentence: two months in prison.

The landowner who had accused her was in the courtroom. When the trial ended, he casually walked up to the judge, shook his hand, and started chatting like nothing had happened.

The next trial was for a stolen samovar. Then a case about stolen timber. Then a group of peasants accused of attacking a district officer.

The Tsar lost consciousness again.

When he opened his eyes, he was in a village. Starving children, shivering from the cold, wandered the streets. A woman, exhausted and overworked, struggled to carry heavy sacks.

Then the scene changed again.

A man was being whipped in a Siberian prison. This was punishment ordered by the Minister of Justice.

Another shift.

A poor Jewish watchmaker and his family were being thrown out of their home because they couldn't pay rent. His children cried, and Isaaks, the watchmaker, looked desperate. After begging, he was finally allowed to stay a little longer.

The Tsar then saw a police chief accepting a bribe. Then a governor secretly taking money under the table. Then tax collectors forcing a poor villager to sell his only cow to pay his debts—while a wealthy factory owner got away without paying anything, thanks to bribing an inspector.

The courtroom appeared again. Another trial. Another sentence. Another punishment. More lashes.

"Ilia Vasilievich, please, have mercy," a peasant pleaded.

"No," the judge said coldly.

The peasant's eyes filled with tears. "Well, I guess that's how it is," he murmured. "Christ suffered, and He teaches us to endure suffering too..."

More scenes appeared before him: a religious group being broken apart and scattered; a priest refusing to marry a Protestant couple and later refusing to bury a Protestant. Orders were given for the Imperial train to pass, forcing soldiers to sit in the mud—cold, hungry, and miserable. Corruption spread through schools and orphanages. A statue was built for someone who didn't deserve it. Church officials stole money. The secret police were given more power. A woman was searched against her will. A prison held convicts waiting to be sent away, while a man was hanged for killing a shop assistant.

Then came the harsh realities of military life: soldiers forced to wear uniforms they didn't respect. A wealthy man's son was excused from service, while the only provider for a poor family was sent to the army. University professors were spared, but talented musicians were forced to serve. Soldiers spread sickness through their reckless behavior.

One soldier tried to escape. Another, who hit an officer for insulting his mother, was sentenced to death. Some refused to fire their weapons and were punished. A deserter was beaten to death in a disciplinary unit. Another, completely innocent, was flogged and had salt rubbed into his wounds until he died. Meanwhile, a high-ranking officer stole money meant for the troops.

The leaders lived in luxury, drinking, gambling, and abusing their power, while the common people suffered—children starving, homes filled with filth, endless work, and hopelessness.

"But where are the people with kindness in their hearts?" the Tsar asked.

"I will show you," his guide said.

He saw a woman in solitary confinement, losing her mind. Another—a young girl—was sick and had been assaulted by soldiers. A man was exiled, left to suffer alone. In a prison camp, women were being beaten. Thousands of good people were locked away, their futures stolen. The younger generation was being crushed by a corrupt system, robbed of any chance to grow into who they were meant to be.

"But what can I do?" the Tsar cried in despair. "I don't want people to be beaten, tortured, or killed! I want everyone to be happy, just as I long for happiness myself. Am I truly responsible for all of this? What can I do to stop it? What am I supposed to do? If I believed even a small part of this was my fault, I would end my life right now. How can I change anything? This is the way the State is built, and I am its ruler. Should I kill myself? Should I give up the throne? But that would mean abandoning my duty. God, help me!" He broke down in tears—and suddenly woke up.

His first thought was relief: "It was only a dream." But as he recalled everything he had seen, he realized the problem in his dream was just as real now that he was awake. For the first time, he fully understood the heavy weight of responsibility on his shoulders, and it terrified him. His thoughts no longer focused on his young wife or the happiness he had planned for that evening. Instead, his mind was consumed by a single, impossible question:

"What am I supposed to do?"

Feeling restless, the young Tsar got up and walked into the next room. There, he found an old courtier— one of his father's trusted advisors—talking with the young Queen, who was on her way to see him. The Tsar approached them and, speaking mostly to the old man, shared his dream and the troubling thoughts it had left him with.

"That is a noble way to think," the courtier replied. "It shows the kindness of your heart. But, forgive me for being honest—you are too good to be a ruler, and you are taking on more blame than you should. Things are not as bad as you believe. The people are not truly suffering; most live well, and those who are poor often bring it upon themselves. Only criminals are punished, and when mistakes happen, they are like storms—rare accidents, or simply the will of God. Your only duty is to rule bravely and protect the power given to you. You want what is best for your people, and God sees that. If you have made mistakes, you can ask for forgiveness, and He will guide you. But in truth, you have done nothing wrong. There have never been rulers as wise as you and your father. So, we ask only one thing: that you continue to lead us, to reward our loyalty, and to trust that, except for troublemakers who do not deserve happiness, your people are already content."

The young Tsar turned to his wife. "What do you think?"

She had been raised in a free country, and her ideas were different. "I see things another way," she said. "I'm glad you had that dream, and I believe you are right to feel the weight of your responsibility. I have thought about it many times, and I think there is a simple way to relieve at least some of the burden. You should share your power with the people by giving them representatives to help govern, while you oversee the bigger decisions. That way, the weight of ruling is not yours alone."

As soon as she finished speaking, the courtier quickly disagreed, and the two began a polite but intense debate.

At first, the young Tsar listened to their arguments. But soon, he stopped hearing their words. Instead, another voice filled his mind—the voice of the one who had guided him in his dream.

"You are not just a Tsar," the voice said. "You are, first and foremost, a human being. You were born into this world only yesterday, and you may leave it tomorrow. Your duty as a ruler, which the old man speaks of, is not the only thing that matters. You also have a greater duty—the duty of a man to his soul, to do what is right before God, to help create a world of justice and kindness. Do not let yourself be ruled by what has always been done or what others expect. Let yourself be guided only by what is right."

He opened his eyes. His wife was waking him up.

Which path the young Tsar chose—whether to listen to the courtier, his wife, or the voice in his heart—would only be known fifty years later.

Thank You for Reading

Dear Reader,

We hope this timeless classic has sparked your imagination and enriched your literary journey. Now that you've turned the final page, we want to share a vision for the future of reading—one where every classic you've ever wanted to explore is at your fingertips, in a format that best suits your life.

We'd like to invite you to gain immediate, unlimited digital & audiobook access to hundreds of the most treasured literary classics ever written—along with the option to secure deluxe paperback, hardcover & box set editions at printing cost. Together, we can spark a new global literary renaissance alongside our small, independent publishing house called "The Library of Alexandria."

Thousands of years ago, the Library of Alexandria stood as a beacon of knowledge—until it was lost to history. We aim to reignite that spirit of preservation and discovery right now, in the modern age—only this time, it's accessible to all, in every language and every format.

Picture a world where every timeless classic, novel,

poem, or philosophical treatise is not only available to read but also updated for today's readers—modernized, translated into any language or dialect, and ready to enjoy in any format you choose, whether that is in an eBook, audiobook, paperback, or deluxe hardcover & box set version a printing cost.

By joining our movement to rebuild the modern Library of Alexandria, you become part of an unprecedented mission to offer:

- **Unlimited Audiobook & eBook Access to the Greatest Classics of All Time**

  Instantly explore thousands of legendary works, from Plato and Shakespeare to Jane Austen and Leo Tolstoy. All are instantly ready to read or listen to, giving you a complete literary universe at your fingertips.

- **Paperback & Deluxe Editions at Printing Costs:**

  Purchase any title in a paperback, deluxe hardbound, or deluxe boxset edition at printing costs, shipped right to your doorstep. Curate your personal library of Alexandria with editions worthy of display— crafted to last, designed to captivate, and delivered straight to your door.

- **Modern translations for Contemporary Readers in all languages and dialects**

  Discover a vast selection of classics reimagined in clear, current language—no more struggling with outdated phrases or obscure references. Next to the original versions, we aim to offer translations in as many languages and dialects as possible.

  As we continue our translation efforts and add new languages, readers everywhere can connect with these works as if they were written today. By bridging linguistic divides, you're contributing to ensuring that these timeless stories become more meaningful, accessible, and inspiring for people across the globe.

- **Your Personal Library of Alexandria:**

  Over the months and years, you'll curate a unique physical archive of classics—each volume a testament to your taste, curiosity, and love of knowledge. It's not just about owning books—it's about curating a cultural legacy you'll cherish and pass down for generations to come.

- **Join a Global Literary Renaissance:**

  Your support fuels an ongoing mission: allowing us to reinvest in offering deluxe print editions (including special boxsets) at their true cost, broaden the range of available formats and translations, and extend the reach of these works to new audiences worldwide. By joining today, you're not just preserving a legacy of masterpieces; you set in motion a powerful wave of literary accessibility.

We are more than a publisher—we're a movement, and we can't do it alone. Your support lets us scale our mission, preserving and reimagining history's greatest works for tomorrow's readers.

Become a Torchbearer of knowledge.

Thank you for picking up this book and allowing us into your literary journey. As you turn the pages, know that you're part of something larger: a global effort to keep these stories alive, share their wisdom across borders and generations, and spark a true cultural revival for the modern era.

If this resonates with you—please consider taking the next step by visiting:

www.libraryofalexandria.com

With gratitude and a shared love of knowledge,

The Modern Library of Alexandria Team

Visit:

www.libraryofalexandria.com

Or scan the code below:

www.ingramcontent.com/pod-product-compliance
Lightning Source LLC
Chambersburg PA
CBHW011518240626
47154CB00010B/3085